Customer Service: 1-877-277-9441 or customerservice@pikidsmedia.com

This publication may not be reproduced in whole or in part by any means whatsoever without written permission from the copyright owners. Permission is never granted for commercial purposes.

Published by Phoenix International Publications, Inc.
8501 West Higgins Road   59 Gloucester Place
Chicago, Illinois 60631   London W1U 8JJ

PI Kids and *we make books come alive* are trademarks of Phoenix International Publications, Inc., and are registered in the United States.

www.pikidsmedia.com

8 7 6 5 4 3 2 1

ISBN: 978-1-5037-5246-7

The illustrations for this book were created digitally, using a tablet, a stylus, and 279 cups of coffee...all held right-side up. Cover design and typography by Sarah Sisterson. Text set in Gilroy.

This Book Is
UPSIDE
DOWN

Written by Erin Rose Wage
Illustrated by Simona Ceccarelli

we make books come alive®
pi kids **Phoenix International Publications, Inc.**
Chicago • London • New York • Hamburg • Mexico City • Sydney

You know something?
I think this book is upside down.

Uh...

Yep.
The words, the pictures, everything.
This book is upside down.

That book is not upside down.
You are upside down.

Oh, brother.

Wrong again.
I am not your brother.

MOM?
I am *certainly* not your mom.
I am a penguin.
And you, my upside-down friend,
are a giraffe.
Totally unrelated.

Oh yeah?
If I were upside down,
could I do...THIS?!

Yes.

Fair enough.
But I still say:
This book is upside down.
So.
How did you get up there, anyway?

I flew.
If you fly up here, too,
I'll prove that book is not upside down—
I, Gus Penguin, give you my penguin's pledge.

But I am a *giraffe*.
And I, Penelope Giraffe,
give you my giraffe's guarantee
—you heard that right,
we giraffes pronounce it
"jarentee" —
I give you my giraffe's guarantee
that giraffes do not fly.
And neither do penguins.

Suit yourself.
Can you gump?
I mean *jump*?

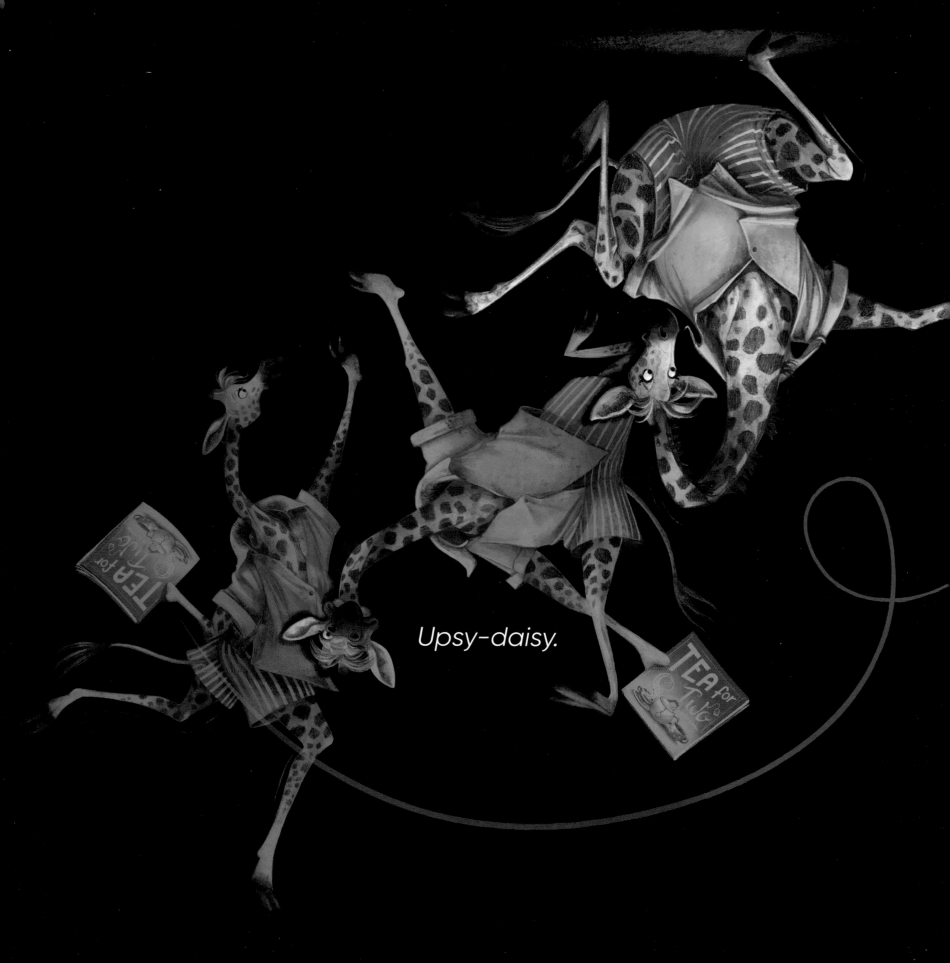

Upsy-daisy.

Maybe you should have
jumped on one foot?

See?
This book is upside down,
and I am right-side up!

That's right.
Did you close your eyes?
I think you need to have at least one eye open.
Or maybe you need one eye closed?

I think I did.
I always lead with my left foot.

My buddy is a lobster.
She knows how everything works.
Hold on a second.
LINDA!

I had one eye open
and one eye closed.

How do you do
that jumping
thing?

I am a lobster.
Lobsters do not jump.
Have you tried
scuttling?

That book is upside down.

I feel kind of funny.
But I am not laughing.

Harrumph.

Ahhhhh.
Oh...
the book.

You know something?
I think this book is upside down.

Uh...

Yep.
The page numbers, the punctuation, everything.
This book is upside down.

That book is not upside down.
You are upside down.

Oh yeah?
If I were upside down,
could I do THIS...